Tessa's Tall Tales

The tall tale always depicts truth as a relative commodity, for the participants in a yarn-spinning performance set the price of confidence.

—*Mark Twain and the Art of the Tall Tale,* Henry B. Wonham, Oxford University Press, USA (January 1, 1993)

Tessa's Tall Tales

Written by Carolyn Joyce Dodds · Illustrations by June Gomez

Published by Byron Hot Springs, San Francisco, California
www.byronhotsprings.com

ISBN: 978-0-578-76211-1

Library of Congress Control Number: 2021938782

Cover and book design and composition by: Leigh McLellan Design

About the Type: Titles and initial letters: Curlz MT, the perfect font for all your fun designs, was designed by Steve Matteson and Carl Crossgrove. *Text:* ITC Giovanni, designed in 1989, by California type designer Robert Slimbach. His goal was to create a face of classic old style proportions that is also thoroughly contemporary. The typeface has a modern feel with a larger x-height for accessibility and ease of reading.

Printed in the United States of America in compliance with the Lacey Act by Ingram® Lightning Source®

For general information and reviews, please contact historian@byronhotsprings.com.

FIRST EDITION

Printed in the United States of America in compliance with the Lacey Act by Ingram® Lightning Source®

10 9 8 7 6 5 4 3 2 1

Disclaimer: All errors and omissions are the responsibility of the author and illustrator.

Follow the adventures of Tessa and all her imaginary friends on her website, http://tessastalltales.com Instagram 	 and 	 Facebook.

To our Wolfpack and the friendships that were formed on the kindergarten playground: the artist, the writer, the card dealer, the high-fiver, the librarian and the "Wolfie" with the musical laugh.

Oh, the tales Tessa tells when
she opens her mouth,

4

burglars and pirates and
trips to the South.

Sightings of spaceships, escapes from the zoo,
she spins stories and falsehoods
and insists they're all true.

She holds court in the classroom,
the kids all amazed.
Tessa loudly describing
events of her days:

toys coming to life and pine trees
heard talking,
dogs driving cars and furniture
walking,

8

dragons in dresses and swimming
with whales,
Tessa never grows tired of telling
her tales.

But oh my, do her mother and father begin
to question and worry about tales she does spin.

Mrs. Wiseowl is even wondering whether, "Has Tessa stopped telling the truth altogether?"

One night before bedtime, Mother and Father agreed,
Tessa needed to learn it's no good to mislead.

As Tessa lay in her bed with warm satisfaction,
Mother and Father put their plan into action.

Father said loudly to Mother just then,
"Saw the Tooth Fairy today.
She looks pretty grim.

She's getting up there in age.
   Fairy's far from her youth.
You know, I'd hate to tell Tessa.
   She's got that loose tooth!

The Fairy's skipping some kids, not visiting all.
She's homebound more often,
    not wanting to fall."

Tessa sprang from her bed, to the hallway she flew.
"Oh Daddy!" she shouted, "Is that really true?"

"Is the Tooth Fairy not coming? Is she really that old?"
"No Tessa," said Father, "That's a tale I just told.

Do you see how it feels when you're not told the truth?"
Tessa felt awful as she wiggled her tooth.

"Your words are important,"
her mother was stern.
"Honesty matters, it's high
time you learn."

20

The tears in her eyes were beginning to glisten,
"Truth is boring," she whispered, "No one will listen."

"Choose what you say wisely."
Father nodded his head,
"You'll earn our respect when
you're honest instead.

22

Your imagination runs wild

and you take us along,

but not knowing
what's real

is most certainly
wrong."

23

Tessa thought of her school, her teacher, her friends.
She wanted to fix this,
to make some
amends.

She agreed with her parents, she knew they were right.
Tessa crawled back in bed and thought deeply all night.

The very next day,
she started anew.
She made the decision
to always be true.

Tessa still tells her stories, every day without fail.
But she always explains, "This is just a tall tale!"

ABOUT THE AUTHOR

Carolyn Joyce Dodds lives in Northern California where she has raised her two grown sons. She is a retired syndicated newspaper columnist and is now passionate about her role as a Special Education Teacher and Reading Specialist. Carolyn has an extensive background as a Behavior Modification Therapist, working with all ages of children and young adults on the autism spectrum. She has served as a strong advocate for families of children with special needs. Carolyn counsels burn survivors through the Alisa Ann Ruch Burn Foundation under the name of "Funshine" and spends her breaks and weekends giving back to the community by volunteering her time to teach life skills, develop social skills and encourage young people to be active through camping, rock climbing, fishing and snowboarding. *Tessa's Tall Tales* is the first in a long line of children's books written by Carolyn. You can learn more about the author at http://AuthorCarolynJoyceDodds.com.

ABOUT THE ILLUSTRATOR

June Gomez is a native Californian. Her artistic talents were nurtured from an incredibly young age. Long road trips were taken with her sketchbook in hand. The cloud formations outside the station wagon window were her first creative inspirations. Soon, June's youthful talents became evident to both her family and teachers. Art and creative projects became her favorite subject in elementary as well as secondary school. Voted "Most Creative" by her high school classmates set the stage for June's four-year artistic journey at the Academy of Art, San Francisco, California. There she earned a bachelor of arts degree in illustration. Today, her professional mural work is prominently displayed in children's rooms, dental offices and commercial spaces around the greater San Francisco Bay Area. *Tessa's Tall Tales* is the second children's book illustrated by June. The first tale entitled *What if Strawberries Had No Hats?* was published in 2019, is written by Cassaundra Brown. This was June's first foray into children's book illustration and now her creative passion. You can learn more about the illustrator at http://MasterpieceMurals.net

Praise for *Tessa's Tall Tales*

As a father of two Tessas of his own, I can say that *Tessa's Tall Tales* holds a special place on our shelf. The wonderfully composed lesson about honesty and personal accountability stands out among the colorful array of children's standards. The freshly voiced message and lesson are equally shared between Tessa and her parents.

—Harry S. Franklin, author of *Paradigm Shift* and *The Time of Madness*

Little wolf Tessa spins her adventures in story form. They unfold in beautiful illustrations and in your heart. She is so creative and captivates you with her tall tales. *Tessa's Tall Tales* is a wonderful book that encourages all of us to use our imagination and, at the same time, not get too carried away. I look forward to more adventures and tales from Miss Tessa.

—Alicia Coleman-Clark, author of *Ava Goes to the Dentist, Ava Goes to the Beach, Ava Goes to the Zoo, Ava Goes to Kindergarten* and *Ava Goes on a Cruise to Mexico*

Have you ever wondered what it is like for a child so full of imagination, who craves attention and views the real world as boring with no one to listen? Meet Tessa, a young wolf cub who tells tall tales of adventure, leaving everyone wondering what is true and what is not. Carolyn Dodds delivers a sweet and poignant story as she brilliantly captures the joy of Tessa, her parents' concerns and the careful way in which they come to a solution without thwarting Tessa's passion and love of storytelling.

—Maribeth Boettcher, retired teacher, Brentwood Elementary School District Librarian and lover of children's stories

CPSIA information can be obtained
at www.ICGtesting.com
Printed in the USA
BVRC100958030921
615978BV00026B/23